D FRAMED FATE

NAMAN NAGPAL

Copyright © Naman Nagpal
All Rights Reserved.

This book has been self-published with all reasonable efforts taken to make the material error-free by the author. No part of this book shall be used, reproduced in any manner whatsoever without written permission from the author, except in the case of brief quotations embodied in critical articles and reviews.

The Author of this book is solely responsible and liable for its content including but not limited to the views, representations, descriptions, statements, information, opinions and references ["Content"]. The Content of this book shall not constitute or be construed or deemed to reflect the opinion or expression of the Publisher or Editor. Neither the Publisher nor Editor endorse or approve the Content of this book or guarantee the reliability, accuracy or completeness of the Content published herein and do not make any representations or warranties of any kind, express or implied, including but not limited to the implied warranties of merchantability, fitness for a particular purpose. The Publisher and Editor shall not be liable whatsoever for any errors, omissions, whether such errors or omissions result from negligence, accident, or any other cause or claims for loss or damages of any kind, including without limitation, indirect or consequential loss or damage arising out of use, inability to use, or about the reliability, accuracy or sufficiency of the information contained in this book.

Made with ♥ on the Notion Press Platform
www.notionpress.com

For those who have danced with chaos, whispered to the stars, and found love within the echoes of their own soul.

Happy Reading

- <3 Naman N

Contents

Foreword

Love, a wild tempest; loss, its quiet aftermath. Between them lies a fragile thread, weaving lives into a dance of longing and letting go. This book is not merely a story but a symphony—raw and resonant, carrying the echoes of hearts that dared to beat too fiercely.

Here, the pages drip with the elegance of midnight cigarettes and half-empty glasses of wine, of whispered words in gilded ballrooms, where chandeliers glimmer like unshed tears. Yet beneath the surface of all that luxury lies the truth the ache of love slipping through trembling fingers, the bruises of choices made in the name of something greater than oneself.

It is not a tale of perfect endings. It is the song of imperfect beginnings and fractured middles, of silences that cut sharper than words and glances that hold the weight of untold stories.

The characters are flawed, achingly human, and within them, you may find fragments of your own heart the part that yearns, the part that breaks, the part that hopes despite it all.

Each chapter hums with poetry, every moment drenched in beauty and melancholy, like the last drop of wine left in a crystal glass. As you wander through their lives, feel the pull of their passions, the sting of their regrets, and the quiet triumph of their survival.

This book invites you to step into its world—not to escape your own, but to understand it more deeply. To remind you that love, in its imperfection, is no less sacred; that even in the shadows of heartbreak, there is a kind of light.

For those who have danced with love and loss, this is for you. A hymn to every scar, every kiss, every tear. *Let it wash over you and leave you changed.*

Preface

"Mann tu jot saroop hai, apna mool pachhan."
"O mind, you are the embodiment of the Divine Light—recognize your own origin."
- ShreeGuru Granth Sahib Ji

This book is a humble ode to the complexities of life woven with threads of love, loss, and self-discovery, all the while standing in the shadow of a truth larger than ourselves. The story of Kavan is like a raag sung softly in the night, echoing across the chambers of the heart, where every note resonates with longing, reflection, and the relentless pursuit of understanding who we truly are.

Kavan's journey is not merely a personal narrative but an exploration of the roles we are **destined to play, the masks we wear, and the truths that we unknowingly bury.** What begins as a tale of mourning and fractured relationships unfolds into a labyrinth of reality and illusion, forcing him to confront questions that go beyond the mundane: **Who am I? Am I the storyteller, or merely a story being told?**

And yet, in his search for clarity, the lines between his world and ours dissolve, urging us to reflect on our own lives. Are we authors of our fates, or simply actors, directed by an unseen hand?

We may struggle through the play of life, guided by unseen hands and mysterious scripts, there is solace in knowing that the true director is the One within—steadfast, eternal, and compassionate.

May this story be more than just a narrative—it is an invitation to question, reflect, and perhaps find peace amidst the unanswered questions.

Welcome to a tale of hearts lost and found, of reality unravelled and rebuilt, and of the light that persists even in the darkest corners of our being.

Prologue

Chandigarh breathed in shadows that night, its skyline aglow with a seductive haze of amber lights and lingering smoke. Somewhere, a jazz melody spilled out of a rooftop bar, its sultry rhythm lost in the velvet fog. I leaned against the window of my penthouse, the glass cool against my fingertips, a half-finished glass of red wine cradled in my hand. The taste of it lingered on my lips dry, bitter, a reflection of the weight in my chest.

The air smelled of rain and faint tobacco, a cigarette still burning in the ashtray beside me. It was hers, the imprint of her absence hanging heavy in the room. I could still see the soul of her in the leather chair by the fireplace, her legs tucked beneath her, her laughter curling in the air like smoke, intoxicating and impossible to hold.

Love, they say, is a luxury. A heady indulgence, much like this wine rich, complex, but prone to turning sour when left untended. Ours had once been a vintage worth savoring, every moment an exquisite escape from the world outside. But now, it felt like a rare bottle cracked open too soon, its flavor not yet ready, its promise wasted.

We had danced in the halls of opulence, her silk dresses whispering secrets as they brushed against my tailored suits. We had shared stolen kisses under Parisian chandeliers and argued under the soft glow of Verona's moon. Love had been a canvas for us, painted in the hues of luxury and recklessness, but somewhere along the way, the colors had begun to bleed.

I picked up her cigarette, the faint imprint of her lipstick still on the filter. I took a drag, the burn sharp in my throat, and exhaled slowly, the smoke twisting into the dim light like the unspoken words that now lay between us.

Ours was not a love that ended in fire and fury. No, it dissolved in the quiet moments the untouched wine glasses, the empty side of the bed, the silence that once held our secrets but now only held our distance.

If love were a luxury, we had both spent recklessly, leaving ourselves in debt to the emptiness that followed.

This is not the story of our beginning. It is not a tale of sweeping romance or grand gestures. This is the story of the cigarette left burning, the wine left unfinished, the love that unraveled not in storms, but in silence.

This is my story. This is hers. This is **ours**. A story of what it means to lose someone you thought you'd never lose, and the taste of love when it turns bitter on the tongue.

CHAPTER ONE

WHISPERS OF YESTERDAY

I closed the door behind Dipanshu, the final click echoing louder in the stillness of the house than I had expected. My body felt heavy, not just from the thirteen days of pooja and rituals, but from the weight of what those days represented. Grief had a strange way of settling in—first like a storm, then as a quiet, persistent ache. The gramophone had gone silent, no longer filling the air with Shazia Manzoor's voice crooning, *"Oh Na Darr Kar Le Mail Dillan Day, Ho Jeunday Rahay Tay Roz Milaan Gay" lines from Chann mere Makhna* (Don't be afraid and meet my heart, if we are alive, we will meet every day) the room felt emptier without it. Without him.

I stretched, trying to loosen the tension in my shoulders, but the sense of absence was palpable. This was the new normal. He wasn't here anymore, and I had to learn to live around that void. We all did.

Radhya had ordered food from the nearby restaurant, but I wasn't hungry. She sat across from me at the table, eyes distant, her mind somewhere else. Yuj was quieter than usual, still not fully understanding the permanence of it all. I turned to Radhya, asking if she had ordered a pack of cigarettes along with the food. She shook her head, lost in her thoughts. I sighed and told her to check on the meal while I went out to fetch the cigarettes myself.

As I stepped outside, the night air hit me—a reminder that life goes on, indifferent to our personal tragedies. From Devsahani Uncle's house next door, I could hear the strains of another song, "*Dard wanda way kehra tere bajon aan kay, Kol na bethay koi menu teri jaan kay*" the lyrics pierced through the still night, a melancholic echo of my own feelings. I forced a smile, a weak gesture of acknowledgment to the universe, and pressed the button for the lift. The silence inside the lift felt suffocating as it descended from the 9th floor to the ground.

Papa's absence was like a shadow, following me everywhere. The memories of him playing with Yuj, caring for him, loving him it was all so vivid, yet so out of reach. He was woven into the fabric of our lives, and now that fabric was fraying.

At the shop, I asked for my usual pack of cigarettes, only to be told they were out of stock. Of course. Even in the mundane, things weren't quite right. After half a mile of walking, I finally found a pack. The weight of it in my hand felt heavier than it should. I pressed the 9th-floor button again, the anticipation of returning to a home that no longer felt like home making my stomach churn.

The smell of food hit me as soon as I opened the door. Radhya had already set the table, but she wasn't eating yet. "I'll have my share after the walk," she said, feeling too stuffed for dinner. I nodded, washing my hands, but the ritual felt hollow without Papa sitting at the head of the table.

We couldn't leave Yuj alone at home anymore he needed both of us now. He had lost his playmate, his guardian. As we got ready for the walk, I held Yuj's small hand in mine, the responsibility heavier than ever. Radhya carried a water bottle, the simple gesture somehow grounding us in the ordinary.

As we stepped out of the lift, Yuj spotted Ivleen, the little girl from next door. He called out a cheerful "Hi," and just like that, the kids were off, playing as if the world hadn't just shifted on its axis. Radhya and I walked in silence for a while, the quiet between us almost sacred.

Then, she broke it.

"I had a strange dream last night," she said, her voice barely above a whisper. "Papa was in it. He was going to some palace. I didn't understand it... and then I woke up."

I glanced at her, my heart tightening in my chest. What did it mean? A palace? Was it a symbol, a farewell, a place beyond our reach? We didn't know. We couldn't know. So we pushed it aside, choosing instead to talk about mundane things, routines we needed to get back to. I had work in the morning, a meeting at the office, and a trip to the ashram to feed the cows. Life needed structure again, even if it felt hollow.

The walk became monotonous, a loop of thoughts and unspoken feelings. We decided to head toward the golf course, though the darkness there was unsettling. Few people walked that path at night, and the stillness there was almost too much to bear. But we did two rounds, just for the sake of keeping the routine.

On our way back, Yuj showed us his new Peppa Pig watch, a gift from Ivleen. He thanked her with a smile so innocent, so unaware of the gravity of loss, that for a moment, I felt lighter. Maybe, in time, we could all feel that way again.

But not yet. Not tonight.

CHAPTER TWO

In the Stillness of Shadows

The following morning, I woke up before dawn, the silence pressing in on me. Radhya lay next to me, her breathing soft, steady, unaware of the looming day ahead. My body still ached from the sleepless nights and the rituals, but I had work to do. The meeting, the cows, and more + grocery too—everything that needed to be done, even when my world had come to a standstill.

Carefully, I slipped out of bed, leaving Radhya in the warmth of her dreams. The house was bathed in the soft, pale blue light of dawn. It's 5:47 AM. I glanced at my phone. I played Shree Ram Amritwani on the gramophone after taking a bath. A stillness settled over everything, the kind of stillness you feel right before the world wakes up, when it's just you and your thoughts. In the corner, Papa's old chair sat untouched, as if waiting for him to return. I lingered for a moment, my hand brushing the worn armrest, and then turned away.

I made my way to the kitchen, took out the planner and started writing the things which I needed to grab from the grocer. I scribbled the tasks for Radhya, glued it on the fridge and started the coffee machine. The scent of the brewing coffee filled the air, momentarily distracting me from the heaviness that sat in my chest. Ah. What a lovely morning it is. Today was just another day, I reminded myself. One more day to get through, in the beautiful words of Papa always said to Mumma, "*Aeh Waqt vi langh jana*" (This too shall pass).

As I sipped my coffee, Radhya stirred awake. She shuffled into the kitchen; eyes still heavy with sleep. "Morning," she said softly, her voice hoarse.

"You slept, okay?" I asked. I hugged her and sooth her back. She pecked and nodded. But that nod was missing with something. I wasn't able to feel the warmth in the air.

She shrugged, leaning against the counter. She exclaimed Kavan, I dreamt about Papa again.

I nodded, unsure of what to say. The dreams... they seemed to be coming to her more frequently now, as though Papa was reaching out, tethered to us by some invisible thread. "What was it this time?" I asked, even though I wasn't sure I wanted to know.

"He was... gardening, it seems the same garden that was of Mrs. Bhatia, lawn swing, white aesthetics, jasmine bushes and a dog" she said, furrowing her brow as if trying to recall the details. He seemed... happy. Peaceful.

I sipped my coffee in silence. "Maybe he's at peace now," I said, though the words felt hollow, like something you say to comfort someone, but not something you truly believe.

Radhya gave me a small, sad smile. "Maybe." I tried to placate her with my hand over her hand.

After a quiet breakfast, we went about our routines. I threw on my work clothes, double-checking my laptop and papers for the meeting. Radhya was busy with Yuj, helping him get ready for school. His little voice filled the space, a welcome contrast to the quiet that had swallowed the house whole. He laughed as he showed off his Peppa Pig watch again. Dadda looked at this dial, it is so bright and colorful. After touching this it will glow in pink dadda, his joy which was an anchor to normalcy.

"We'll drop him off on my way," Radhya said, her hands busy packing his school bag and went straight to restroom. Meanwhile I Double checked his things, pencils done, crayons done, bottle done, tiffin done. I guess I'm missing something.

A loud voice all the way from the lobby to the room came, Kavan the eraser is placed on the right side of the bed. I replied in a strong voice. Okay.

We left our *Saanidhay* ; the house, locked it. Safar from floor 9 to ground again in lift.

I nodded, grateful for the help. "Thanks. I'll head to the office after I stop by the ashram."

By the time we were both ready to leave, the sun had climbed higher in the sky, casting the world in a harsh light that didn't match my mood. Yuj skipped ahead of us to the car, blissfully unaware of the weight we carried. He was a child his world still simple, unburdened by loss. I envied him for that.

As Radhya and Yuj drove off, I made my way to the ashram. The drive was short, but my mind wandered back to the last time Papa had come here with me. He had loved this place, the quiet serenity of it, the way the cows would gather around him as if sensing his calm presence. Feeding them was something we'd done together for years, a tradition I had no intention of breaking, even now.

The ashram was quiet when I arrived, the cows gathered in the distance, their gentle mooing the only sound. I grabbed the bag of feed from the back of my car and walked over, feeling the sun warming my back. As I scattered the feed, a strange sense of peace washed over me. For a brief moment, I could almost feel Papa beside me, his hand on my shoulder, his voice in my ear telling me, *"Puttar ki hoya, me ethe hi haiga twade naal, guru maharaj vi haige ne mere naal, me khush aa"*. But it was just a fleeting thought, gone as quickly as it came.

With the feeding done, I sat on one of the stone benches nearby, letting the stillness seep into me. Life had changed in an instant, yet in places like this, the world continued to move at its own pace, unchanged by the chaos in our hearts.

I stayed there longer than I intended, lost in thought. It wasn't until my phone buzzed

It was a Team's reminder for the meeting in the next 15 minutes, and I snapped back to reality. I rushed back to the car, the spell of the ashram broken, and drove toward the office.

The office, no it is YYF, was a world away from the quiet serenity I had just left. It's a playground of rats, technically corpo-rats. As I stepped into YYF, the hum of teams and outlook, the buzz of conversations plainly gossips, and the sharp ring of phones jolted me back into the present. Colleagues offered sympathetic glances, a few even murmured condolences as I passed by. I gave them a tight-lipped smile, the kind that said, "I appreciate it, but please don't ask me how I'm doing."

The meeting was mercifully short thankfully, but my mind was elsewhere. I went through the motions, nodded when necessary, and said the right things. The way his absence seemed to follow me, even here, in the midst of deadlines and emails.

After the meeting, I sat at my desk, picked up the Rubik's cube and started juggling it, staring at the screen without really seeing it. A colleague knocked softly on the cubicle wall. “You alright?”

I blinked, forcing myself back to the present. “Yeah, just... adjusting.”

He nodded, understanding in his eyes. “It takes time.”

“Yeah,” I replied, though I wasn’t sure how much time it would take. Or if time would ever be enough.

The rest of the day passed in a blur, the hours slipping away unnoticed. By the time I got home, the sun had already begun to set, casting the world in hues of orange and pink. Radhya and Yuj were in the living room, a quiet scene of normalcy that felt almost too fragile. Again the gramophone was not playing Shazia I glared at.

Yuj ran up to me, his face beaming. “Dadda! Look, I drew this at school today!”

He held up a crayon drawing, a jumble of colors and shapes. “That’s Kavan Dadda, and Radhya Mumma, and it’s me, Yuji!” he exclaimed proudly.

I knelt down beside him, forcing a smile. “It’s perfect, Yuj. Absolutely perfect.” Hearing this he was on cloud nine.

As I hugged him close, I felt the weight of the day pressing down on me again. Papa may be gone, but in moments like this, in the laughter of my son, in the warmth of Radhya’s gaze, there were echoes of him everywhere.

CHAPTER THREE

Beneath the Veil of Secrets

I leaned back in Papa's chair, trying to shake off the weight of the day. The night had settled in, thick and heavy, as if it was trying to smother the daylight. The house was unusually quiet, save for the faint ticking of the wall clock. My eyes fell on the window, the curtains swaying gently as if stirred by something more than just the evening breeze.

I played a Ghazal "Rafta Rafta" by Mehndi Hasan Saabh and was wondering how beautifully he penned down each word together forming this masterpiece. To be honest, each word was exceptionally brilliant and heart wrenching.

Something felt off, but I couldn't quite put my finger on it.

The melody of Radhya's lullaby drifted through the half-open door, a gentle balm against the quiet of the night. "*Bhaut raat beeti, chalo mein sula doon*" (It's been a long night, you should sleep), she sang, her voice as soft as the touch of Yuj's tiny hand against her cheek. I could see her silhouette in the dim light, her movements deliberate yet tender, a choreography of motherhood. Yuj stirred, his lashes fluttering once before stilling, the innocence of sleep claiming him. I should have felt peace contentment, even but instead, a strange weight pressed against my chest, insistent and heavy.

I leaned against the doorframe, my gaze caught between them and the darkness pooling outside the window. A father should feel safe watching his family cocooned in such love, yet tonight, the stillness felt ominous. The walls seemed to close in, their silence too thick, the shadows too alive. My mind was elsewhere, snagged on a single thread, unraveling and fraying in the space between her lullaby and my own thoughts.

It was Praan's message—the one I had stared at for far too long earlier tonight—that stirred this unease. His words were ordinary, almost curt, yet they bristled with an undercurrent I couldn't name. A father knows when something isn't right. It's an instinct, the same one that tells you to hold your child's hand tighter near a busy street or to check if they're still breathing when the night gets too quiet. And tonight, that instinct was a scream muffled by the calm exterior of routine.

I should have been with them, lost in the warmth of the moment, but instead, I was caught in the cold grip of something unnamed and unshakable.

I'm coming over tomorrow. We need to talk. About something important.

That was all it said, and Praan wasn't the type to send cryptic messages. I was not really sure what the topic would be. Not unless something was really wrong. As I'm a bit of an overthinker so that thought was constantly lurking around in my brain.

Praan and I had always been close, from wearing the same Old Rock T Shirts to attending the concerts together. Back in our childhood we used to make scrapbooks of Cars and Stationary items. But there was a part of him I could never fully understand. He had always been a bit secretive, more reserved than I was. Totally, into himself. He loves to hang out alone and enjoys being in solace. Even now, as he built his life with Ishita, his fiancée, there were still things he kept to himself. Like keeping the phone to himself and charging it in the bathroom, No phone touch policy. But this message... It wasn't like him. There was an urgency in it that unsettled me.

The next morning, I woke up to the sound of footsteps in the hallway. For a brief, disorienting moment, I thought it was, but I chuckled the thought. But as reality settled back in, I realized it was Praan, arriving earlier than expected. It was just a quarter past eight in the morning. He had a habit of doing that showing up unannounced. Praan being Praan.

When I opened the door, Praan stood there, his face drawn and serious. Behind him, Ishita lingered, her usual smile replaced by something more guarded. Her eyes flicked toward Praan as if she was waiting for him to speak first. Ishita greeted me, Hello Bhaiya. We exchanged greetings.

"Kavan," Praan said, his voice low, almost urgent. "Can we talk?"

I nodded, I said Praan just come inside, make yourself feel comfortable. Yes, we'll talk. Is everything fine, I asked.

As soon as they crossed the threshold, I sensed the tension between them. Ishita's gaze flicked around the room, avoiding eye contact with me. Radhya, sensing something off, took Yuj out to the park, giving us space. I asked Radhya to bring some Tulsi Leaves for the next day's pooja. It will be Ekadashi. She said, yes.

"Let's sit," I said, leading them to the living room. The air felt thick with unsaid words as they settled on the couch, Ishita keeping a deliberate distance from Praan.

Praan leaned forward, his hands clasped together, knuckles white. "I don't know how to say this, Kavan, but... I need your help."

I studied his face, the seriousness in his eyes. "What's going on?"

He exchanged a glance with Ishita, who gave him a subtle nod as if granting him permission to proceed. Praan took a deep breath.

The three of us sat in Papa's old study, a room heavy with the weight of untold stories. Ishita sat by the window, her silhouette illuminated by the flickering city lights, while Praan leaned against the oak table, his hands fidgeting with a stray thread on his sleeve.

You remember Ganesh Visarjan, Kavan? Praan broke the silence, his voice carrying an unusual tremor. The one where I disappeared for hours? Outskirts of the city?

I looked up, surprised. He had mentioned it before, in passing, like a trivial anecdote. But now, the way his words hung in the air made my chest tighten. Yeah, you said it was a special occasion or something. Praan gave a hollow laugh, shaking his head. "Special? That's one way to put it." He paused, the air between us thickening. It wasn't just Ganpati Visarjan. I went there looking for something... or someone.

The shift in his tone was undeniable. I leaned forward. "Someone?"

His gaze darted to Ishita, who turned her face away as though bracing herself. "Her name is Saadhika," Praan said finally, each syllable like a weight falling into place. The name struck something deep within me, a faint echo of familiarity I couldn't place. "Who is she?"

Praan hesitated, his Adam's apple bobbing as he swallowed hard. "She's... may be related to us."

For a moment, the world stilled. The hum of the ceiling fan, the distant honks of the city, even the steady rhythm of my breath—all of it faded. "Our what?" I whispered, barely able to form the word. Praan ran a hand through his hair, exhaling shakily. Because I found her. At Ganpati Visarjan. She sent me a letter, asking me to meet her there. I didn't tell you because... because I didn't know how to.

"A letter?" I repeated, my mind catching on the word.

Praan nodded. "No signature. Just a few cryptic lines and a place to meet. At first, I thought it was some prank, but then I saw her. She had Papa's eyes, Kavan. There was no mistaking it.

"And?" I pressed, my voice sharp. "What happened?"

Praan's face darkened, his hands trembling. She wasn't just there to meet me. She wanted answers. She wanted to know about Papa, i really dont know why. A cold shiver ran down my spine.

She's back, Praan whispered, his eyes wide, haunted. And she's not just looking for answers anymore. She's angry, Kavan. Angry at all of us.

Ishita, who had been silent, suddenly stood. This isn't just about her being angry, is it? she asked, her voice trembling. There's something more. Something you're not saying.

Praan avoided her gaze, his shoulders slumping. The letter she sent me—it wasn't just a message. It was a warning. And it had... a symbol. What symbol? I asked, though part of me already knew the answer.

Praan met my eyes, and for a moment, we were kids again, standing by the riverbank during Ganpati Visarjan all those years ago. It was the same symbol we saw carved into that tree. The one we promised never to talk about.

The memory hit me like a tidal wave. The summer evening, the carvings on the tree, the eerie silence that followed us home. We had chalked it up to childish imagination, burying the fear deep inside. But now, it was clawing its way back to the surface. You think Saadhika's connected to that? I asked, my voice barely steady.

I don't know, Praan admitted, rubbing his temples. But the symbol in her letter—it's identical.

I stood, pacing the room as my mind raced. The pieces were falling into place, but the picture they formed was something I wasn't ready to face. We need to go back, I said finally, my voice resolute. Back where? Ishita asked, her confusion and concern evident. To the riverbank, I said, meeting Praan's eyes. To where it all started.

Praan nodded slowly, his dread mirrored in my own. Ishita looked between us, her jaw tightening. You're not going without me, she said firmly. I wanted to argue, but the determination in her eyes left no room for debate. And maybe, just maybe, we'd need her strength for what lay ahead.

As we prepared to leave, I couldn't shake the feeling that this wasn't just about Saadhika. It was about the secrets we had buried, the promises we had broken, and the reckoning that was finally upon us.

And deep down, I knew that going back to that riverbank wouldn't just bring answers. It would change everything.

CHAPTER FOUR

THREADS WOVEN BY FATE

I called Radhya from the park. I explained the whole story and She was discombobulated by the whole incident. She can't connect the dots of the happenings. I hugged her and said, we really need to help Praan.

She put the leaves on the table, and asked me to dip them in water. I filled the vessel with water and then dipped them. They can survive now.

The drive to the riverbank felt like a journey back in time. The memories of that place had lain dormant for years, it was a wholesome nostalgia of Ganpati Visarjan buried under the weight of work, life, and family. We were in the place which once made us all happy. But now, with every mile we travelled, they began to stir again, like ghosts roused from slumber.

Radhya sat beside me, her hand resting lightly on mine, her calm presence grounding me. In the backseat, Praan was unusually quiet, his gaze fixed on the window, lost in thoughts he wasn't ready to share. Ishita, sensing the tension, leaned into him, her head resting on his shoulder. There was a sense of helplessness in between the two but the two stood by themselves. They seemed closer now, their love of silent reassurance against the shadows of the past.

As we pulled up to the riverbank, the familiar landscape came into view unchanged, like a snapshot frozen in time. The trees lined the bank just as they had all those years ago, their branches whispering in the wind. It was here, beneath one of those very trees, that we had found the symbol.

I turned off the engine and stepped out, the cool breeze hitting my face. Praan followed, his steps hesitant, as though he were walking into a place haunted by something he couldn't quite name.

Radhya and Ishita lingered behind, watching us. "We'll give you both some time," Radhya said softly, giving my hand a gentle squeeze. I smiled at her, grateful for her understanding.

Praan and I approached the tree, the weight of our shared history pressing down on us. It felt strange, standing here again after all these years. A part of me had always wanted to forget that night—the way we had stumbled upon the strange carvings, the way the air had felt charged with something we couldn't explain.

“There,” Praan whispered, pointing at the tree's base.

The symbol was still there, faded but unmistakable. A series of three interlocking circles, each one etched into the bark with precision. It was the same symbol from Saadhika's letter. The same symbol we had once seen, back when we were too young to understand what it meant.

“We were just kids,” I said, my voice thick with memory. “We didn't know what this was.”

Praan knelt down, tracing the outline of the circles with his fingers. I always thought it was just some prank, something left behind by teenagers or travellers. But after

Saadhika's letter... I don't know, Kavan. I started to wonder if there was more to it.

"Saadhika's gone now," I said, my tone more certain than I felt. Whatever connection she had to this, us and all... it's over. That was our past and Ishita is your present. So, whatever was there in the letter it is kind of a hallucinating act.

Praan stood up, brushing the dirt from his hands. Maybe. But the symbol—it's still here. And there's something else you should know. He hesitated, glancing back toward Ishita as if unsure of how much to share.

Radhya was quietly observing the place. She is deciphering the dots which probably she once noticed as I can read her mind. She was not comfortable at that moment.

As soon as I stepped to placate her, she said in a fierce voice.

"Papa knew about this place." Radhya replied to all four of us, raising eyebrows.

I stared at her, caught off guard. "What do you mean?"

"He used to come here, even before death." Radhya continued. I found an old journal of him after he passed in that trunk. He wrote about this riverbank and Ganapati Visarjan. About finding the same symbol carved into the trees.

I took a step back, the weight of Radhya's words sinking in. "Papa was here? Why didn't he ever tell us?"

"I don't know," Radhya admitted. But it feels like this symbol... It meant something to him. Like it was part of something bigger. Something he didn't want us to know about.

The realization hit me like a wave, knocking the breath from my lungs. Our father, the man who had always been our anchor, had secrets. And those secrets were tied to this place, to this symbol.

As the wind rustled through the trees, I found myself staring at the symbol with new eyes. What had Papa been involved in? What had he hidden from us all these years?

Before I could dwell on the questions, Ishita and Radhya walked over, their faces lit by the soft glow of the afternoon sun. Radhya's presence, always a source of comfort, steadied me. Radhya said, Chuck it. Bygones be Bygones.

She slipped her hand into mine.

"Yeah," I replied, forcing a smile. "Just... old memories."

Ishita looked between me and Praan, concerned etched in her expression. "What now?"

Praan hesitated, then shook his head. We let it go. Saadhika's gone, and whatever this was... it's in the past now. I don't want it to follow us into our future. Probably Saadhika was a subconscious reminder to us for the reminiscent memory of Papa.

I nodded, sensing that he was ready to close this chapter of his life. "Agreed. Let's move on."

We walked back to the car in silence, but the atmosphere had shifted. I played Bayaan the whole journey back. The darkness that had hung over us seemed to lift, and for the first time in weeks, I felt lighter, as though a burden I hadn't even realized I was carrying had been lifted.

A song adds *"Roz-o-shab, rangon ki, Khoj mein rahay, Har lamha, yaado ki, Mauj mein bahay, Din Dhalay, Shaam ho..."* and I can totally relate to it.

That evening, after we returned home, I found Radhya sitting on the balcony. I asked her to pass the ashtray. Hoof. It's a long day, Radhya. The glow of the Chandigarh's street lights reflecting in her eyes. She looked peaceful and content. I joined her, slipping an arm around her shoulders. Radhya comforted me by playing my favourite song over gramophone

"You've been quiet," I said gently.

She smiled, leaning into me. "Just thinking about how far we've come."

I nodded, understanding what she meant. These past few weeks have been hard—losing Papa, uncovering old secrets, and the strange events surrounding Praan's past. But in the midst of it all, Radhya and I had found something solid, something unbreakable in each other. The glaze in Radhya's eyes was making me calm.

"How's Praan?" she asked. I turned my head to the left and her eyes flicked toward the living room, where he and Ishita were curled up on the couch, talking in hushed voices. All we can hear is some lovey dovey stuff and we put on the earplugs.

"I think he's finally ready to let go," I said. Whatever happened with Saadhika, it's in the past now. And he's got Ishita. She's good for him.

Radhya smiled. They seem happy together. You can see it in the way they look at each other.

I watched them from a distance, the way Ishita's hand rested on Praan's arm, the way he leaned into her, his face relaxed for the first time in days. Their love had weathered the storm, and now, it was growing stronger. They'll be alright, I said, my heart lighter than it had been in weeks. And us? Radhya asked, her voice soft but calm.

I turned to her, my hand gently brushing her cheek. We're better than alright. Radhya smiled and we kissed. Thankfully there was no gramophone but it was the wind chime which is adding the flavour to the evening.

Ah, in that moment, as the city hummed around us, and the cool night air wrapped us in its embrace, I realized how lucky I was. Despite everything—the loss, the confusion, the mystery Radhya and I had found our way back to each other.

And as for Papa's secrets, they could stay buried in the past. What mattered now was the future. A future filled with love, with family, and with the promise of new beginnings.

CHAPTER FIVE

LOVE'S SILENT SYMPHONY

It was the D-Day, the festivities began as Ishita and Praan are getting married soon. Well, to be very precise I can't keep calm specially when your younger brother- super secretive brother is at the peak moment to get married.

The evening was perfect—cool breeze, soft music, and the golden glow of fairy lights draped across the lawn. I can see a placard printed #Ish_ke_Praan, I burst out with laughter. Radhya was like what was that? Kavan. I hilariously replied, Ish ke Praan. I found it quirky and funny. The event planners these days are so creative and quirky with their ideas. It was Praan and Ishita's pre-wedding party, and the air was filled with a sense of joy, anticipation, and love. Everyone had gathered at the beautiful garden venue by the hillside, where laughter mingled with the scent of blooming jasmine. It was a resort kind of setup where everyone stayed for one and a half days to celebrate their big day. It was a closed knitted affair.

Radhya and I stood near the entrance, watching as friends and family danced under the shade of twinkling lights. I could see Praan and Ishita across the lawn, over there on the mosh, stealing glances at each other like lovestruck teenagers. Aww cute. Tonight was theirs; a night to celebrate the love they had fought so hard to protect.

"*Zara unhe dekho*," Radhya whispered, smiling as she nudged me. They're glowing.

I followed her gaze. Praan looked more alive than I had seen him in weeks, his arm wrapped protectively around Ishita's waist. She was radiant in a pastel blue dress that caught the light as she twirled, her laughter ringing out like music.

Okay, so the Pastel Blue dress is the show stealer. It was a bespoke couture from a local designer of Italy. That designer, was friends with Praan's college mate, Naaz Walecha. He designed it on the very next day of our confirmation. The design was the hardest part to choose from five different designs. Well of course that decision was led by Ishita. She was indeed looking pretty.

I glared at them and said "They deserve this," my heart was full for them.

The evening unfolded with ease. Guests were making toasts, laughter was constant, and Praan and Ishita couldn't keep their eyes off each other. In the midst of it all, I caught a moment to slip away with Radhya.

"Let's take a walk," I suggested, nodding toward the winding path that led into the hills.

She smiled knowingly. "You always want an adventure."

"Just a short one," I promised, taking her hand as we sneaked away from the party.

We walked hand-in-hand through the garden, the sound of the celebration fading into the background. The stars were bright overhead, and for a moment, it felt like we were the only two people in the world.

You know," I said after a while, "I never thought we'd be here. Not like this, after everything that happened.

Radhya leaned her head on my shoulder. But we are. And that's what matters.

We stopped at a secluded spot on the hillside, overlooking the valley. Below, the lights of the town twinkled like stars. It was peaceful, the kind of peace that comes after a storm. I kept my hand on her cheeks, she blushed. That smile gave me a sign of possibility. We hugged each other and the best part happened.

"Kavan," Radhya said softly, breaking the stillness. "There's something you should know. About Saadhika."

I turned to face her, surprised by the shift in her tone. "What is it?"

She hesitated for a moment, then said, "She's not just someone from Praan's and yours past. She's your step-sister."

The words hit me like a punch. "What?"

Radhya nodded; her expression serious. It's the truth. Your father; he had another family before you and Praan. Saadhika is from that family.

Radhya told the whole background of it to me. When we came back from the riverside. The very next day Radhya was on the walk to a nearby park. There she had an encounter with Uncle Devsahani. They exchanged greetings and he asked how everything was going on and Radhya explained the whole story. Uncle was a bit hesitant to tell as Uncle and Papa were very close to each other. They're like childhood best friends.

The one statement of Uncle, "Saadhika was their sister." Yes, Radhya. She was their step sister.

For a moment, the world seemed to tilt. The past few weeks suddenly made more sense the strange connection between Saadhika, the symbol, and our father. The reason why she had shown up in their life with so much intensity.

"But why didn't Papa tell us?" I asked, my voice barely a whisper.

Radhya sighed. I don't know. Maybe he thought he was protecting you both. Maybe it was too painful for him to talk about.

I let the truth sink in. Saadhika wasn't just some mysterious figure from our past. She was part of our family a sister we had never known. But now, with her gone and her chapter closed, I realized it didn't change anything. She had chosen to stay in the shadows of our lives, and now, we were moving forward without her.

Back at the party, the music had slowed down, and couples were on the dance floor. The DJ played the OG song of all time, "Ae meri Zohra Jabeen". I found Praan and Ishita, standing under a canopy of flowers, lost in their own world. They must be from the world of Anuv.

I approached them, pulling Praan aside for a moment. There's something you need to know, before tomorrow. He looked at me, confused but patient. "What's going on?"

I took a deep breath. "Saadhika... She's our step-sister." Hehe

The words landed with a quiet finality, and I watched as Praan processed the truth. His eyes flickered with understanding, then with something like relief.

"Step-sister?" he repeated, almost to himself. "I guess that makes sense."

I nodded. It's why she was so tied to us, to Papa. But she's gone now, Praan. And her chapter is over. Sigh of relief.

Praan looked over at Ishita, who was watching us with a soft smile on her face. He turned back to me, his eyes clear and focused. He said, "I don't really know how to react to Kavan but this picture, what's happening now is my future, stating her eyes on Ishita and everyone and I am not in any mood to spoil this for the mistakes of past or having any regret. But can we do one thing to gel up the thing, if we can invite her too, still ceremony is pending and guestes are coming".

I patted him on the shoulder, proud of him. "That's all that matters."

The rest of the night was nothing short of magical. As the music picked up again, Praan and Ishita were pulled into the centre of the dance floor by their friends, and soon enough, the whole party was dancing. Radhya and I joined them, laughing and spinning under the stars.

At one point, someone brought out sparklers, and soon, the garden was lit up with tiny bursts of light, everyone holding one and waving them around like children. Praan and Ishita danced through the sparks, their laughter echoing through the night. It was the kind of joy that felt endless. Yuj gave a special performance for his best Chachu, which got appreciated by everyone and Praan hugged him tightly.

As the night wore on, we all gathered around a bonfire that had been set up at the edge of the lawn. People sat on blankets. I could see Bhua, Chachu, Uncle-Aunty, Mama-Mami all together, roasting marshmallows and telling stories. The best storyteller of our family was Suman Uncle. He was an OG standing there undefeated. His laughter and giggles filled the whole ambience into a mirthful venue. I watched as Praan and Ishita sat together, her head on his shoulder, his arm around her, the firelight flickering across their faces.

"I think they're going to be alright," I said to Radhya, who was leaning against me, her eyes half-closed in contentment.

She smiled sleepily. "They're more than alright. They're perfect."

I couldn't help but agree. This was the beginning of something beautiful, not just for Praan and Ishita, but for all of us. We had come through the storm, and now, we were standing in the sunlight.

As the fire crackled and the last of the sparklers burned out, I looked around at the people I loved, and I knew that this; this moment was all we needed.

The ballroom hummed with the rhythm of clinking glasses and soft laughter, but Kavan's phone buzzed insistently in his pocket. He stepped out onto the terrace, leaving behind the golden glow of chandeliers.

"Rujhaan," Kavan greeted, leaning against the cold metal railing. "Calling from Canada, huh? Couldn't resist a good party you're not invited to?"

On the other end, Rujhaan's laugh was deep and familiar. "What can I say? I have a sixth sense for your drama, bro. How's the evening?"

Kavan sighed, glancing at the crowd through the glass doors. "It's... complicated. Family, emotions, the usual."

Rujhaan paused. "You sound like you're carrying the weight of everyone in that room. Remember, Kavan, not every fight is yours to solve. Sometimes, letting people be is the best you can do."

Kavan frowned. Easy for you to say. You're living in your serene Canadian bubble with Natasha.

"She says hi, by the way," Rujhaan teased. And Prakrut does too.

The mention of Prakrut made Kavan stiffen. “Prakrut?” Yeah. Natasha mentioned they’re working on some project together. Small world, huh?

“Too small,” Kavan muttered, before quickly changing the subject.

CHAPTER SIX

IN BETWEEN THE PAGES

As soon as Kavan learned and told the the truth about Saadhika, he immediately asked Radhya for her contact and dialed her number without hesitation. Saadhika answered, her voice cautious and unfamiliar, not recognizing him at first as she was driving back from the office. With a sense of urgency, Kavan extended an invitation an impromptu plan formed in the eleventh hour. He decided to leave the venue and personally bring her to the event, sensing that this meeting deserved a moment beyond introductions.

Kavan requested Radhya to oversee the arrangements for Saadhika's arrival, urging her to return to the party and enjoy the evening with everyone else. Radhya nodded, trusting his judgment, as Kavan stepped out, anticipation building with every passing moment.

At 10:47 PM, The ballroom's dance floor glowed under chandeliers that cast a warm, golden light over the crowd, reflecting off sequined dresses and crisp tuxedos. Laughter and clinking glasses filled the air, but for Kavan, the celebration felt strangely distant a moment dipped in anticipation and laced with something unspoken. This night was meant to honour Praan and Ishita's love, but beneath the surface, a shadow lingered, tugging at the edges of Kavan's mind.

Praan and Ishita glided across the dance floor; their steps so perfectly attuned they seemed to melt into each other's rhythm DJ played, Behke Behke. Watching them, Kavan felt a pang he hadn't allowed himself to feel in years. Perhaps it was a memory of a time with Radhya, family and with himself too; a love he thought he'd understood, yet now seemed as distant as the stars. Across the room, Radhya leaned into Kavan, her laughter rich but tinged with an unfamiliar freedom, as though she had shed something he was only beginning to understand. A part of him wanted to look away; another part, the one that knew things were changing irrevocably, wanted to watch.

And then there was Saadhika, drifting in and out of the night's warmth like a silent spectre. Her eyes found his across the room, and in them was a familiar shadow, a weight she had carried alone until now. Something in her presence quiet, yet unignorable drew Kavan into her orbit. She was the last remnant of his father, the keeper of secrets Kavan hadn't known existed, the part of his family he had never seen fully.

As the evening wore on, she approached him, her voice nearly swallowed by the hum of music. She looked at him, gaze steady, intense, a truth hanging between them like a delicate thread.

"Praan," she whispered, her voice barely carrying above the music. "It's time you knew." She hesitated, her eyes dark with the weight of unspoken words. "I'm your sister. Papa... he was my father too."

Kavan replied positively mentioning about Uncle Devsahani.

The room seemed to fade neutral around him, the lights dimming, sounds dulling. Praan's world tilted, his father's legacy splitting into something he could barely comprehend. All his life, he had chased his father's approval, a ghost he could never quite grasp, yet here was Saadhika, a reflection of that same chase—a chase that had only been half the story.

"I always thought..." He struggled for words, his voice taut. "It was just us. You, Praan, and I."

Saadhika's gaze softened, as if she understood that this revelation wasn't just about family, but about the pieces of herself she'd been searching for his entire life. "We're family, Praan. Not in the way you thought, maybe... but that doesn't change what we are." She paused, her voice tinged with a sadness she hadn't seen before. "This was the last secret he kept. Maybe he wanted to tell you, but he couldn't. Maybe he thought it was better this way. I had to tell you, for both of us."

For a long moment, Praan couldn't speak. Here, in the middle of this glittering ballroom, the ground had shifted. He had been lost, searching for something he didn't know, while the answer had been quietly waiting in the form of this sister he had only known at a distance.

He looked at Saadhika, trying to hold onto the fragments of anger and confusion, yet beneath them was a strange calm, a relief he didn't understand. It wasn't a forgiveness, not yet, but it was a beginning—one that had been waiting for this very moment.

As the night waned, Kavan appeared, his laughter buoyant as he pulled Praan back into the celebration, blissfully unaware of the storm that had passed between his brother and his newfound sister. Praan returned to the gathering, but his gaze kept drifting to Saadhika. She was a part of him now, bound by blood and the complexities of a hidden past.

Later, as the guests began to filter out, Saadhika caught his eye one last time, a small, knowing smile tugging at her lips. She nodded, a silent farewell. With that, she drifted into the night, a whisper of his father's legacy, a part of the family that could never be untangled, yet one that might always remain just out of reach.

And as she left, Kavan felt both the weight and lightness of a truth finally known—Saadhika's presence lingering like an echo, an answer that had opened something within him, even as it slipped quietly away.

CHAPTER SEVEN

CRACKS IN THE GLASS HEART

Kavan couldn't shake the weight of Saadhika's revelation. She was his sister another truth hidden in the web of his father's secrets, woven quietly into the edges of his life, waiting to be uncovered. Even as the party roared on, he felt a strange emptiness settle in. How much of his life had been built on things he didn't know?

Returning home that night, the streets blurred past him, his thoughts drifting between the fragments of his family's past and the echoes of his present. He felt disconnected, like a man watching his own life from a distance, powerless to change it.

But as he stepped into his quiet apartment, the reality of another fracture awaited him, the next morning.

Radhya your phone was ringing. She asked who it was. It's 981... To that she said to hang it up. I scrolled left. Radhya came from the bathroom, picked up her phone in haste and looked confused. I went straight for the bath as our times were clashing, it's already 9:45 in the morning and pancakes were on the table.

There was a strange thing happening between both of us, these days we're not giving time because of unprecedented meetings, appraisal acknowledgements and too much work stress.

The tension between Radhya and I had been simmering for weeks, barely beneath the surface, like an electrical charge waiting for a spark. It started innocuously, small disagreements over trivial things; dinner plans as I reserved a table for two at Parikrama the revolving Bistro bar but she's not able to make up for it, also it involved house chores, or how late I stayed at work—but it was growing into something deeper. Something I couldn't quite name yet, but I could feel it pressing against my chest.

Coming back from the office, I thought of carrying our favourite Hazelnut Custard Apple ice cream. I bought two of them and one chocolate orange for Yuj. He's so fond of it.

I arrived home late. Yuj was asleep and Radhya was on the verge of sleep. I murmured the words, "Ice Cream laaya hoon, get up". Her reaction was as cold as frozen ice cream. She asked me to keep it in the refrigerator.

Radhya had changed. I couldn't ignore it any longer. Her energy had shifted, becoming unpredictable, almost erratic. Every little thing seemed to annoy her these days—whether it was a misstep in my words or an innocent question about her day. She was sharp, her words biting at me when I least expected it.

It was as if we were walking on two different paths, ones that had started close but we're slowly diverging. And in the middle of it all was the stress of our careers.

For weeks, I had been drowning in work, trying to juggle my growing responsibilities at the office. I felt like I was constantly under pressure to deliver, to prove myself. The late-night calls, the last-minute projects—it all piled up, leaving me with little time for anything else. Meanwhile, Radhya's own career was taking unexpected turns. We both were growing but on our own terms. She had taken on more projects, expecting the NYC project would be a glimmer to her career. She became absorbed in something that I couldn't quite place my finger on.

One fine evening when we're having our dinner of monotony and silence. This time the gramophone got replaced by the laptop's speaker uttering the sound of Teams Notification, constant emails and the MOMs: the deployment week.

You're never home anymore, Radhya said one evening, her tone sharper than usual as she placed the dinner plates down with a little too much force.

"I'm working," I replied, trying to keep my voice steady. You know how demanding the office has been. We have a new client coming in next week, and I—. It's always work with you, she snapped, cutting me off. You never have time for us.

I paused, setting my fork down, frustration bubbling up. And what about you, Radhya? You're barely around either. We haven't had a proper conversation in days.

Radhya glared at me, her eyes flashing. I'm doing my best. My projects matter too, Kavan. You act like your work is the only thing that's important.

That's not what I'm saying, I sighed, rubbing my brows. I'm just saying we're both occupied, and we need to figure this out.

Her lips tightened into a thin line, and for a moment, I thought she was going to yell. But instead, she stood up abruptly and walked out of the room, leaving me sitting alone at the table, my appetite gone.

Days passed, and things didn't get any better. Radhya became more distant, occupied, her mood unpredictable, and I found myself constantly on edge around her + super occupied too. Every conversation felt like a minefield, with me tiptoeing around, afraid of triggering yet another argument.

The day for the final submission, Client was there in YYF. I need to get things sorted. I double checked the emails, presentations, off server checks and certainly the voice of mine.

I heard a tinge on my notification window, popping up an email from the Delivery Manager subject with "Congratulations Kavan, We made it."

Another mail from the client side too, appreciating my work.

Drum roll, 3...2...1... Prakrut entered the picture, the same guy who is working with Natasha, Rujhaan's beloved.

Prakrut was a colleague, college mate and best friend of Radhya's, someone she had mentioned in passing a few times before. I hadn't paid much attention at first, assuming he was just another coworker. But lately, his name has started to come up more often. Radhya talked about him casually, slipping him into conversations here and there—how helpful he was, how they worked well together.

And then, one evening, I saw them together.

I had left work early, hoping to surprise Radhya with dinner and a quiet night in, something to break the growing tension between us. But as I walked into the restaurant, I saw her sitting at a corner table with Prakrut. They were laughing, her hand casually resting on his arm, the kind of easy familiarity I hadn't seen between us in weeks.

Something inside me twisted.

I watched them for a moment, frozen in place, my mind racing. Was I imagining things? Was I being paranoid? Or was this something more?

When Radhya finally looked up and saw me standing there, her smile faltered, and for the briefest second, I saw something in her eyes guilt, or maybe surprise. She quickly stood up, trying to play it off.

"Kavan," she said, walking toward me, I didn't expect to see you here.

I nodded, glancing at Prakrut, who was still seated, watching us with a raised eyebrow. Neither did I.

It's just a work dinner, she explained, her tone too casual, too rehearsed. We were, We were discussing the project.

I nodded again, my stomach in knots. "Right."

I didn't say anything more, but the seed of doubt had already been planted.

The following days were a blur. Radhya's mood became more volatile, and I found myself slipping into a dark place. Every time I saw her on her phone, yes it was Prakrut 981 the digits I saw on her phone, every time she mentioned a work meeting, I couldn't shake the image of her with Prakrut. It was eating away at me, a growing insecurity that I couldn't control.

I became obsessed with small details—where she was going, how long she was gone, who she was with. I literally acted like a finicky husband. I knew it was unhealthy, knew I was driving myself insane, but I couldn't stop. I started checking her messages, of course they were filled with 981 digits, when she wasn't looking, trying to find the legit traces of something more between her and Prakrut. Had spotted them thrice or four times together sharing the depth of moments on the name of work meetings.

“Kavan, what’s wrong with you?” she snapped one evening when I confronted her about yet another late night out. “You’re acting paranoid.”

“Am I?” I shot back, my voice rising. “Maybe if you were actually honest with me, I wouldn’t have to be.”

She crossed her arms, her expression cold. Honest? You’re accusing me of something that isn’t even happening. Prakrut is just a friend, Kavan. But he definitely knows me better. It’s not like we’re into each other but we know each other really well. You’re making this into something it’s not.

“Am I?” I repeated, my voice shaking with anger. Then why do you spend more time with him than you do with me?

Radhya’s face twisted with frustration. Because he listens, Kavan. Because when I’m around him, I don’t feel like I’m constantly walking on eggshells.

Her words cut deep, but I couldn’t stop myself. So that’s it, then?

She didn’t respond immediately, and the silence felt like a punch to the gut. When she finally spoke, her voice was quieter, almost resigned.

I don’t know what I feel anymore, Kavan.

That night, I slept on the couch, my mind spinning with doubt and anger. I had become finicky, paranoid, insecure, but I couldn’t help it. The cracks in our relationship were widening, and I didn’t know how to fix them.

CHAPTER EIGHT

The Cradle of Distance

The night was unusually quiet, as if the city itself had taken a pause to mock the silence in my home. I sat at the dining table, staring at the untouched glass of wine in front of me. The hum of the refrigerator was the only sound that filled the room. It was maddening.

Radhya was in the bedroom, the faint rustle of her moving around reaching me like a whisper of something I'd already lost. I wanted to get up, to go to her, but my legs felt rooted to the chair. What could I even say?

For weeks, something between us had been unraveling. Slowly at first barely noticeable. A missed conversation here, a quick goodbye there. But now, it felt like we were standing on opposite sides of a canyon, shouting into the void, hoping the other would hear.

I glanced at the wall where our photo hung—a candid from the early days. We were laughing, her head thrown back in that carefree way I'd always loved, my arm draped over her shoulder like I could protect her from anything. I stared at the photo, willing it to give me answers.

Where had that gone?

I grabbed my phone, scrolling through old messages, my chest tightening with every swipe. The early ones were full of life: "**Can't wait to see you!**" "**Guess what happened today?**" But as I scrolled, the words became shorter, colder: "**Don't forget Yuj's project.**" "**I'll be late.**" By the time I reached the most recent messages, they were nothing more than logistical updates.

Somewhere along the way, I'd stopped noticing the little things—her favorite tea, the way she'd hum when she was focused, the silence she needed after a long day.

And maybe, just maybe, she had stopped noticing me too.

In the bedroom, I found her sitting on the edge of the bed, folding clothes with a precision that felt almost aggressive. She didn't look up when I walked in.

"Radhya," I said softly.

Her hands didn't stop moving. What is it, Kavan?

I hesitated. I wanted to tell her everything—that I missed her, that I was scared, that I didn't know how we'd gotten here. But all I managed was, "I miss us."

She froze for a moment, her hands clutching the fabric in her lap. Then she looked up at me, her eyes glistening. "Do you?" she asked, her voice barely above a whisper. Or do you miss the idea of us?

Her words hit me harder than I expected. I stepped closer, sitting on the bed beside her. "I don't know," I admitted. "Maybe both. But I do know that I hate this. I hate feeling like I'm losing you."

Her laugh was bitter, a sound I didn't recognize. You lost me a long time ago, Kavan. You just didn't notice.

I felt the air leave my lungs. "I thought I was building a future for us. I thought that's what you wanted."

"I wanted **you**," she said, her voice breaking. "Not just a provider. Not just a husband who shares the bills and schedules. I wanted the man who used to make me feel like the center of his world."

Her words cracked something inside me. I wanted to argue, to defend myself, but deep down, I knew she was right. I don't know how to fix this, I said finally, my voice barely above a whisper. "But I want to try."

She shook her head, a tear slipping down her cheek. "Trying isn't enough, Kavan. You have to choose. Every day. Every moment. You have to choose us, even when it's hard, even when it's inconvenient."

Her words echoed in my mind long after she left the room.

That night, I lay on the couch, staring at the ceiling. Memories played in my head like a film reel: the day we met, our wedding, Yuj's first laugh. Every moment that had brought us here, to this point, where everything felt so fragile.

I thought about what she'd said—about choosing. Wasn't that what I had been doing? Working late nights, taking on bigger responsibilities, all to build a life for us? But maybe I'd gotten it wrong. Maybe what she needed wasn't the house or the future I was building. Maybe what she needed was me.

When morning came, the light filtering through the window felt cold. I sat up, my body aching from a restless night.

As I walked into the bedroom, I saw her packing a small suitcase.

"Radhya," I said, my voice shaking. "What are you doing?"

She didn't look at me. "I need some space."

"Space?" My heart pounded in my chest. "What does that mean?"

She zipped up the suitcase, her hands trembling slightly. "It means I need to figure out what I want. I can't keep pretending everything is okay."

"What about Yuj?" I asked, desperation creeping into my voice.

Her shoulders tensed. "I'll come back for him later."

I stood there, watching her as she walked past me, her footsteps heavy but determined. The door closed behind her with a soft click, and I was left alone in the silence.

I sat down on the edge of the bed, my head in my hands.

I didn't know how to fix this. I didn't even know if it was fixable. But as I sat there, the weight of her absence pressing down on me, I made a decision. If there was even a shred of hope left, I would fight for it.

Not with words or promises, but with actions. With the quiet, consistent presence she had always deserved.

I just hoped it wasn't too late.

and the journey, from being strangers to strangers again, was beautiful.

CHAPTER NINE

HER INNER WORLD

Her Inner World: Through Kavan's Eyes

Radhya had always been a mystery to me, a beautiful enigma wrapped in strength and vulnerability. Even in our most intimate moments, there was a part of her she kept hidden, a fortress around her heart that no amount of love could breach. I admired her for it, for her resilience, but over time, I realized it wasn't resilience. It was survival.

She carried the weight of her past, childhood like an invisible chain, one forged long before I met her. It shaped her decisions, her fears, and, ultimately, the way she loved.

My own childhood wasn't all that different from hers. My father was a man of principles like a typical indian man, his expectations as rigid as the lines of his ledger books. He loved in the only way he knew by providing, by building walls of rules and discipline. My mother, on the other hand, was a beacon of softness, but she was often overshadowed by his sternness.

I grew up tiptoeing around his temper, my every achievement scrutinized, my every mistake magnified is this the new concept, No. There was no room for vulnerability in his house. Well, Vulnerability is the bigger emotion, no space for being upfront. Emotions were weaknesses, and weaknesses were not tolerated. Putting point of views was considered as arguing and not discussions.

As a child, I had learned to suppress my feelings, to bury my insecurities beneath a façade of confidence. I thought I had left it behind, but when I met Radhya, I realized how much of that little boy still lived inside me the one desperate for validation, for connection, for love that didn't feel like a transaction.

Radhya and I were two broken pieces trying to fit together, but instead of healing each other, we only seemed to deepen the cracks.

Radhya's past was etched in her silences, in the way she avoided certain topics, and in the haunted look in her eyes whenever her father's name came up. She had grown up in a house where love was conditional, tied to achievements and appearances.

"I was never enough for them," she once told me. "No matter what I did, there was always something I lacked. My father wanted perfection, and my mother wanted peace. I could never be both."

She carried that belief into every part of her life her career, her relationships, even motherhood. She pushed herself relentlessly, chasing an ideal she couldn't define, trying to prove her worth to a world that didn't even ask her to.

And I blind in my own wounds didn't see how much it was costing her.

Radhya's need to prove herself clashed with my need to feel needed. I wanted to be her anchor, her safe place, but she saw *safety as a cage*. I wanted her to lean on me, to let me in, but she had spent her whole life learning that vulnerability was a luxury she couldn't afford.

My childhood had taught me to crave reassurance, to seek validation in others. Hers had taught her to depend on no one but herself. Together, we were a storm—two opposing forces crashing against each other, both desperate to be understood but too afraid to show our true selves.

I saw it in the way she threw herself into work, taking on projects that left her drained but fulfilled some unspoken need. I saw it in the way she avoided my touch, not out of malice, but because intimacy scared her. And I saw it in the way she connected with Prakrut; a man who seemed to understand the parts of her I couldn't reach.

One fine night, as we lay in bed, I tried to talk to her about it.

"Radhya, do you think we're happy?"

She turned to look at me, her eyes soft but guarded. "Happiness is fleeting, Kavan. Maybe we're just... functional."

"Is that enough for you?" I asked, my voice cracking.

She didn't answer. Instead, she reached for the bedside lamp, plunging the room into darkness.

That silence spoke louder than words.

Her past had taught her to guard her heart, and mine had taught me to fight for it. But the more I fought, the more she retreated. It wasn't that she didn't love me she did, in her own way. But her love was shaped by a lifetime of lessons that told her love was fleeting, conditional, fragile.

And I desperate for reassurance pushed too hard, demanded too much. My need for validation clashed with her need for space, and neither of us knew how to bridge the gap.

We were both prisoners of our pasts, carrying the weight of childhood wounds that neither of us had truly healed from. Her fear of being controlled collided with my fear of being abandoned, creating a cycle of misunderstandings and unmet expectations.

The night she told me she needed space, I felt the ground shift beneath me.

"I'm not leaving you," she said softly, her eyes glistening with unshed tears. "But I need to find myself, Kavan. I can't do that here."

"Find yourself?" I repeated, my voice hollow. "What does that even mean?"

"It means I need to figure out who I am outside of this—outside of us."

Her words cut deep, but they also carried a painful truth. We had been so focused on trying to make each other whole that we had forgotten to heal ourselves.

As I watched her pack her bags, my mind drifted back to our first days together—the laughter, the passion, the promise of a future built on love and trust. How had we gotten here? How had we let our pasts dictate our present?

I wanted to beg her to stay, to promise her that we could fix it. But deep down, I knew that wasn't the answer. We were two broken people trying to build something whole, and until we confronted our own demons, we would only keep tearing each other apart.

That night, as the door closed behind her, **I realized that loving someone isn't always about holding on. Sometimes, it's about letting go** about giving them the space to heal, even if it means breaking your own heart in the process.

CHAPTER TEN

THE OCTOBER RAIN

I was coming back from the YYF. As soon as I stepped in, I played the radio. It's the show of RJ Sharmeen, She's the one who unveils the horoscopes in a little quirky manner. The paradigm shift in my playlist is a significant direction to my life, who it is unfolding. Sharmeen said, "To all my Scorpio darlings, it is high time to introspect and have faith in Sache Patshah." These two lines soothed me. I was calm, driving and enjoying the harmonious solace.

The house felt hollow.

After Radhya left, the silence was deafening. I can't hear Yuj coming running screaming Dadda. I had never noticed before how much space we filled together our conversations, the soft clink of mugs in the morning, her laughter, even our arguments. Now, without her, the walls seemed to close in on me, amplifying every creak, every shuffle of my footsteps. I would sit on the edge of the bed at night, staring at the place where she used to sleep, wondering how we had fallen apart so completely.

But this wasn't just about Radhya. It was deeper than that.

Papa's absence was something I had buried for so long, pretending I was okay, that I could keep going. But grief doesn't work that way. It sits inside you, quietly pondering at your heart, waiting for the right moment to crash through your defences. Losing him was like losing a part of myself, and now, losing Radhya felt like the rest of me was unravelling.

I tried to fix things. I really did.

I pinged her on WhatsApp, sent messages to Radhya, trying to explain, trying to apologize. But every time I typed something out, the words felt shallow, they were not doing justice to the situation, like they weren't enough to convey the weight of what I was feeling. I asked her to come back, to talk, to try again. She responded, but her replies were cold, distant, as if she had already made her decision.

Dry texts we shared for quite a few days.

"Hi."

"Hello."

"Supp?"

"I'm good, getting ready for work, talk to you later."

I even showed up at Tanishq's place once, hoping that seeing me in person would remind her of what we had—of who we were. But the door stayed closed, and the silence on the other side told me everything I needed to know.

She wasn't coming back.

A similar situation to Atif Aslam's song *Tere Bin* was happening to me for real.

I started walking. I don't know why or where, but every evening, as soon as work ended, I would find myself outside, wandering the streets. The city lights blurred into a haze, the sounds of traffic and distant laughter fading into white noise as I walked for hours, hoping that somehow, the movement would shake something loose inside me.

Days after Radhya left, my phone lit up with a text from Rujhaan.

"Heard what happened. Call if you need to talk."

I ignored it at first, but by midnight, the suffocating silence of the apartment pushed ME to dial.

"She's gone," I said, his voice breaking as soon as Rujhaan picked up.

"Gone, like left-left?" Rujhaan asked, concern lacing his tone.

I swallowed hard. "Packed a bag, said she needed space. I can't... I don't even know what I did wrong."

Rujhaan sighed. "Kavan, this isn't about right or wrong. It's about understanding where it all broke down. Did you listen to her, really listen? Or were you too busy fixing things to notice what she actually needed?"

The words hit me like a punch. "I... thought I was trying."

Sometimes trying isn't enough if it's not in the right direction, Rujhaan said gently. Look, I'm not saying it's all on you. But maybe this is a chance to figure out your part in it, you know? Without blame—just clarity.

and that conversation went to four thirty in the morning. Rujhaan was such saviour.

One evening, I ended up at a Hanuman Mandir.

I hadn't been to a temple in years. Spirituality was always something I felt connected with.

But standing in front of the Mandir now, I felt a pull a need for something beyond myself, something I had ignored for far too long. I walked inside, taking a small vial of Jasmine oil, silver foil (Chaandi Work) and Sindoor (Vermillion) along with the soft hum of Hanuman Chalisa echoing through the hall.

I didn't know what I was looking for, but I sat down, closed my eyes, and let the quiet wash over me. I prayed to Baba. The noise in my mind, the endless spinning thoughts of Papa, Radhya, and my own failures they began to fade, replaced by a deep, aching sense of loss. Baba's vicinity is the best one can ever sense and feel.

The way Baba used to guide us, the way he made everything feel right, even when life was falling apart. And now, without Papa, I felt adrift—like a ship lost at sea, with no compass to bring me home.

Tears slipped down my cheeks, and for the first time in months, I started howling like a newborn baby. I didn't wipe them away. I let them fall, let the grief pour out of me in a way I hadn't allowed since the day we lost him. I was legit crying, seeking for clarity, composure and peace from my Baba.

"Baba, Hanuman ji" I whispered, my voice breaking in the empty hall. "I don't know what to do."

The days blended together after that. I threw myself into nine to five, teams, notifications, emails, trying to distract myself from the ache of everything I had lost. I went to conferences, completed tasks, even went out for a hangout with colleagues, pretending that everything was normal. But it wasn't. It never would be again.

Every time I returned home, the weight of the empty apartment crushed me. I would sit on the couch, staring at my phone, willing it to buzz with a message from Radhya. But it stayed silent. And each day that passed made it harder to hold onto hope.

I tried to fix myself, too. I started reading about mindfulness, spirituality, self-realization—anything that could pull me out of this pit I had fallen into. I meditated, though I was very naive at this, forcing myself to sit in silence and confront the storm of emotions swirling inside me. Guided meditations from YouTube literally came as a survivor.

At first, it felt impossible. My mind raced, my chest tightened, and all I could think about was how broken everything was. But slowly, over time, something shifted. The noise in my head didn't go away, but it softened, just enough for me to breathe through it.

I began to realize that the problems between Radhya and me weren't just about her and Prakrut. They were about me, too—about the insecurities I had buried, the fear of not being enough, the constant pressure to prove myself, both at work and in our relationship. I had pushed her away, little by little, without even realizing it. And by the time I noticed, it was too late.

One night, I tried calling her again. I don't know why—maybe I thought I still had a chance to explain, to fix things.

"Radhya, Radhya, please," I said, my voice shaking as I left yet another voicemail. "I'm sorry. I messed up. I didn't mean to push you away. I just... I don't know how to be without you."

The line went dead, and I stared at my phone, waiting for a response that never came. Never say never I said Kavan, It's alright.

The truth was brutal: I couldn't fix it. No matter how much I tried, no matter how many times I apologized or explained myself, I couldn't go back and undo the damage that had been done. I couldn't erase the hurt, the misunderstandings, the distance that had grown between us.

And I couldn't bring Papa back.

Loneliness became my constant companion, chuddy buddy types. I went back to the same Hanuman Mandir, a few more times, seeking solace in the quiet, trying to find answers in the stillness. But the ache of loss stayed with me, a permanent part of who I was now.

It was in those moments of silence that I began to understand something deeper about myself—about life. No matter how much we try to control things, no matter how hard we fight to keep the people we love close, some things are beyond our control. Loss is inevitable. Change is inevitable.

But maybe that was the point. Maybe, instead of trying to hold onto everything so tightly, I had to learn to let go. To trust that, even in the chaos, even in the heartache, there was something greater at work. Something I couldn't see yet, but that I had to believe was there.

Weeks passed, and the pain didn't go away, but it dulled. I stopped calling Radhya. I stopped expecting her to walk back through the door. Instead, I focused on myself—on healing, on accepting the things I couldn't change.

One evening, as the sun set and the city was bathed in golden light, I sat on the balcony, breathing in the cool air, puffing up my cig. For the first time in a long time, I felt a strange sense of peace. Not because everything was okay—it wasn't—but because I was learning to live with the pain, to accept it as part of my journey.

I wasn't fixed. I wasn't healed. But I was moving forward, step by step baby steps, into the anonymous.

And for now, that was enough.

CHAPTER ELEVEN

TRIUMPHS DRAPED IN TEARS

Lately, I was dealing my best with loneliness and an email broke the silence of life. Well, to sum it up, I got nominated for the GMA awards 2024. GMA I can't imagine, it is the Mecca of Corporate People.

The applause echoed through the hall, louder than I had expected. I stood on stage, holding the glass trophy that felt heavier than it should. Employee of the Year, Kavan Sukhija—it was the accolade I had been working toward for months, the validation that my late nights and sacrifices had been worth something.

Camera crew asked for a smile and along with my colleagues and the presenter I borrowed a fake smile on my visage. But as I smiled for the camera, my mind drifted far from the celebration. The cheers sounded distant; the congratulatory handshakes almost mechanical. Everyone around me seemed genuinely happy for me, but inside, I felt hollow.

The weight of the trophy in my hand didn't compare to the weight of everything else I had been carrying. There I can't count the things happening.

After the GMA, I stepped outside the venue to catch my breath and to have a few puffs to placate the jitters of life. The cool night air hit my face, grounding me for a moment. I should have felt proud, elated even. But all I could think about was how much I wished things were different.

My phone buzzed in my pocket— I scrolled down from the lock screen window, an email from work. I ignored it and leaned against the railing, closing my eyes. I thanked Baba.

But on the contrary, the truth was, no award, no recognition, no professional success could fill the void left by the crumbling pieces of my personal life.

Then I saw her.

Across the street, in a small café Layla, Radhya was having the same macaroons and mascarpone cheesecake with the 981 guy. She was laughing, her head thrown back in a way I hadn't seen in months. The smile on her face was genuine, her eyes sparkling. And as much as it hurt to admit, she looked happy. They looked happy.

I watched them from a distance, my heart tightening in my chest, almost to burst. I had known for a while that things between us were over, that whatever bond we once had had been frayed beyond repair. But seeing her like this with Prakrut made it all too real. This was the closure I hadn't wanted to accept.

I took a deep breath, trying to steady myself. There was no bitterness in me, no anger, just a deep, aching sadness. Radhya had moved on. And as much as it hurt to see her with someone else, a part of me knew she deserved happiness. Even if it wasn't with me.

Later that week, I took Yuj on vacation to Yas Island. It was something we had planned for months, but now, as we boarded the plane, I felt the weight of the trip settle heavily on my shoulders. Yuj was excited, bouncing in his seat, chattering about all the rides he wanted to go on, the things he wanted to see. His energy was infectious, but beneath it all, I couldn't shake the exhaustion I felt—emotionally and physically.

It wasn't easy being a parent when your own world felt like it was falling apart. Yuj was still too young to understand what was going on between Radhya and me. He just knew that things had changed that Papa wasn't around as much and that Mama was always tired.

As we arrived at the island, I tried my best to focus on him, to be the father he needed. We spent the days exploring theme parks, riding roller coasters, splashing in the pool. Yuj's laughter was constant, and for a while, it was enough to keep me present in the moment.

But every time I looked at him, I saw Radhya. He had her eyes, her smile, her energy. And no matter how hard I tried to push it away, the thought of her of us was always there, lingering at the edge of my mind.

One evening, after a long day of activities, Yuj fell asleep in the hotel room. I stood by the window, staring out at the lights of the island. The sounds of the ambience faded into the background as my thoughts consumed me. I missed her. I really miss her every day. I missed the life we had built together—the late-night talks, the walks, the plans we made for the future, the way we used to laugh over the smallest things. But that life felt like a distant memory now, something I could never get back.

And then there was Prakrut.

Seeing them together had forced me to confront the truth: Radhya had moved on, and I hadn't. I was still holding onto something that no longer existed. We had tried to fix things—tried to talk, to rebuild—but every attempt ended the same way: in frustration, in misunderstandings, in failure.

We were both too broken to repair what had been lost.

The next morning, Yuj and I went to the beach for a cleaning campaign "Beach Please!". He was full of excitement, running along the shore, collecting seashells and dragging me into the water. For a moment, watching him play, I felt a sense of peace a fleeting moment of happiness in the middle of the chaos. We sat on the sand as the sun began to set, Yuj nestled against my side. He talked about everything and nothing, his little voice filling the silence I had grown so used to.

"Dadda, do you miss Mama?" he asked suddenly, looking up at me with his Radhya's, innocent eyes.

I got nervous, feeling the familiar lump in my throat. "Yeah, buddy," I said softly. "I do."

He nodded, as if that was all the answer he needed, and turned back to the ocean. The line from "*Humari adhoori kahani*" swung to my brain, watching the waves roll in. I wished I could protect him from all of this from the confusion, the pain, the inevitable questions that would come as he grew older. But there were some things I couldn't shield him from.

Later that night, after Yuj had fallen asleep, I lay in bed, staring up at the ceiling. The events of the past few months played over and over in my mind—losing Radhya, seeing her with Prakrut, the endless pressure of trying to be everything for everyone. I felt like I was being pulled in a million different directions, being anonymous in my own world, trying to keep it all together while slowly unravelling inside.

And then, in the quiet of the night, I whispered a question I had been holding inside for far too long.

"Why is it so hard to be a man?"

The words felt heavy in the stillness of the room. I didn't know who I was asking—the universe, Papa, myself. But it was a question that had been eating away at me. The pressure to be strong, to be the provider, to be the one who held everything together—it was suffocating. I had been taught my whole life that men weren't supposed to show weakness, that we were supposed to handle everything with stoicism and control. But I was tired.

Tired of pretending that I had it all figured out, tired of keeping my emotions locked away, tired of trying to live up to an expectation that felt impossible to meet. I had lost Radhya, I was barely holding onto my relationship with Yuj, and no amount of professional success could fill the emptiness I felt inside. At that moment, I felt small—like a boy again, looking up to Maa-Paa, wishing they were here to tell me what to do, how to handle this weight. But they weren't here. And I was left to figure it out on my own.

The next day, Yuj and I packed our bags and headed back home. The trip had been a brief escape, but the reality of everything I was dealing with loomed large as we boarded the plane.

As we flew back, I held Yuj's hand, watching him sleep peacefully beside me. He was my anchor, the one constant in all the chaos. No matter what happened between Radhya and me, no matter how broken I felt, I knew I had to be there for him.

Maybe I didn't have all the answers.

Maybe being a man wasn't about having it all together or never showing weakness. Maybe it was about showing up, even when it was hard.

Maybe it was about love, even when everything else was falling apart.

And as the plane soared through the clouds, I closed my eyes and whispered one more question to the universe, hoping for a sign, a sense of clarity.

But all I got in return was silence.

CHAPTER TWELVE

Cigarette Conversations

The night was heavy with a quiet stillness, the kind that makes you acutely aware of your own breathing. The inner ground stretched before us, a shadow of its former glory, cloaked in darkness save for the faint shimmer of starlight above. It felt both familiar and foreign, a relic of a time when life seemed simpler, yet somehow more profound.

The cricket ground looked smaller than I remembered. It felt like a lifetime ago when Rujhaan and I used to sit on this very field, dreaming about futures that were supposed to be simpler than the tangled realities we lived now. The floodlights were off, the stands empty, and the grass damp with dew. Above us, the stars sprawled, indifferent to our insignificance.

Rujhaan had come back from Canada a week ago, and when he called me tonight, his voice carried something heavy—something familiar. We'd always been good at reading between each other's silences, and this one was screaming for the kind of conversation you could only have under the cover of night, with cigarettes as your only witnesses.

When I arrived, he was already there, leaning against the old bench near the boundary line. A cigarette hung from his lips, and his expression was half-hidden in the glow of his lighter.

“Still on Canadian time?” I joked, trying to lighten the mood as I approached.

He smirked, exhaling a cloud of smoke. “Still on Canadian problems. Sit down, man.”

I dropped onto the bench beside him, and he offered me a cigarette. I took it, even though smoking wasn’t really my thing. Tonight wasn’t about habits or health. It was about needing something—anything—to dull the edges.

“So,” he began, his tone casual but his eyes sharp. “What’s going on with you?”

I took a drag, the smoke burning my throat. “Radhya left.”

His face didn’t change, but I saw the flicker of understanding in his eyes. He nodded slowly, letting the silence settle before speaking. “Why?”

I laughed bitterly. “Why does anyone leave? She said she needed space. Said she couldn’t figure herself out with me around. But I think... I think she was already halfway gone before she even packed her bags.”

Rujhaan leaned back, staring at the stars. “Doesn’t mean it hurts any less, does it?”

“No,” I admitted, my voice cracking. “It doesn’t.”

For a while, we just sat there, the night pressing in around us. The stars seemed farther away than ever.

“You know,” he said finally, “Inara asked about you the other day.”

I raised an eyebrow. “Inara? Your girlfriend?”

He nodded. "She's been working with Prakrut on some big project. Said she heard about what's been happening with Radhya."

Hearing Prakrut's name was like a slap to the face. I'd been trying not to think about him, about how his name always seemed to linger in Radhya's conversations, about the way she'd laughed with him in ways she hadn't laughed with me in months.

"What did she say?" I asked, trying to keep my voice steady.

"Nothing much," Rujhaan said, taking another drag. "Just that he's... around a lot."

I clenched my fists, the cigarette nearly snapping in my hand. "You think there's something going on between them?"

Rujhaan shrugged. "I don't know, man. But that's not the point."

"Then what is?"

"The point," he said, turning to face me, "is that you're so focused on him that you're not even looking at yourself. You think this is just about Prakrut? Or about Radhya? It's bigger than that, Kavan."

I looked away, the weight of his words pressing on my chest. "What do you mean?"

He sighed, leaning forward, his elbows resting on his knees. "Look, you and Radhya—you're both carrying shit you've never dealt with. And instead of working through it, you're just piling it on top of each other."

I frowned, his words striking a nerve. "What's that supposed to mean?"

"It means," he said, his voice firm, "that you've been so busy trying to fix her that you haven't even noticed how broken you are."

I opened my mouth to argue, but the words caught in my throat. He wasn't wrong.

"I get it," he continued. "You love her. You want to be there for her. But Kavan, you can't pour from an empty cup. And right now? You're running on fumes."

His words cut deep, and for a moment, I couldn't speak.

"You know what Inara told me once?" he said, his voice softer now. "Love isn't a chain that holds tight; it's the wind that lifts the soul higher. It's not about possession it's about freedom. True love doesn't ask for control; it surrenders with grace, allowing each heart to wander and grow. When it's meant to be, love returns not as a promise, but as a masterpiece, richer and more beautiful than ever before. Sometimes, it's about letting go. Not because you don't care, but because you care enough to let the other person figure out their own shit."

I stared at him, my throat tight. "And what if she doesn't come back?"

He shrugged, his expression unreadable. "Then you figure out how to be okay without her. You figure out how to be you, Kavan. Not Radhya's boyfriend, not her savior. Just you."

The words hung in the air, heavy and undeniable.

"Do you ever feel like..." I started, then hesitated.

"Like what?"

"Like you're scared to be alone?"

Rujhaan looked at me, his gaze steady. "Of course. Everyone is. But you know what's scarier? Losing yourself in someone else. That's a hell of a lot harder to come back from."

The honesty in his voice cracked something open in me, and before I knew it, the tears were falling. I turned away, embarrassed, but Rujhaan just sat there, smoking his cigarette like nothing had happened.

"Men can cry, you know," he said after a while, his tone lighter. "Doesn't make us any less manly."

I laughed through my tears, the sound raw and unsteady. "Thanks, Dr. Phil."

He smirked, flicking his cigarette into the grass. "Anytime."

As the night wore on, we talked about everything and nothing our childhoods, our fears, the futures we used to dream about. He told me about Canada, about Inara, about the ways he'd almost screwed things up but managed to claw his way back.

When the first rays of dawn began to break, painting the sky in shades of lavender and gold, we sat in silence, watching the world come alive again.

"You'll be okay, Kavan," he said finally, his voice quiet but firm. "Maybe not today, maybe not tomorrow. But you will be. Just don't lose yourself in the process."

As I watched him walk away, his silhouette fading into the morning light, his words stayed with me, lingering like the taste of smoke on my tongue.

I didn't have all the answers yet, but for the first time in a long time, I felt like I was starting to ask the right questions.

CHAPTER THIRTEEN

FALLING APART

The house echoed with its emptiness, a cavern of silence punctuated only by the occasional creak of wood or the distant hum of traffic. Radhya's absence was no longer jarring; it had settled into the spaces she left behind, filling the air like an invisible presence I couldn't escape.

Yuj's laughter used to drown out the quiet, but even that had grown faint these days. He sensed it too—the unspoken tension, the weight of what was lost. Children always know, even when you try to shield them from the storm.

One evening, I came across her scarf, forgotten and draped over the back of a chair. It smelled faintly of, jasmine and something uniquely Radhya. I held it for a moment, letting the memories rush in unbidden. The way she'd laugh at the smallest jokes, her relentless energy when we first moved into this house, how her eyes would light up when she talked about her dreams.

But now, all of it felt distant, like something I'd watched from behind a glass screen, unable to reach.

I thought about calling her, asking her to come back. But what would I even say? Words felt inadequate, flimsy against the tidal wave of everything that had happened between us. I knew she wouldn't answer, and if she did, I wasn't sure I could handle the coldness in her voice.

Two days later, she showed up at the house. Unexpected, unannounced.

"I came to pick up a few things," she said, avoiding my eyes.

"Of course," I replied, stepping aside to let her in.

She moved through the house with a purpose, collecting books, clothes, and small trinkets she had left behind. Watching her was surreal. It was like seeing a stranger inhabit the shell of someone you once knew intimately.

As she packed, I wanted to say something, to reach out, but the words caught in my throat. The air between us felt heavy, charged with all the things we weren't saying.

Finally, I couldn't hold it in. "Radhya, do you ever think about what we used to be?"

She paused, her hands hovering over a stack of books. "All the time," she said quietly.

"Then why does it feel like we're letting it slip away?"

She looked at me then, her eyes filled with a sadness so profound it made my chest ache. "Because sometimes love isn't enough, Kavan. Sometimes, people grow in different directions, and trying to force them back together only causes more pain."

Her words hit me like a blow, but deep down, I knew she was right.

That night, after she left, I sat in Yuj's room as he slept. His small face was peaceful, untouched by the chaos swirling around him. I stroked his hair gently, tears burning the corners of my eyes.

How did we get here?

Days turned into weeks, and the silence became a companion. Radhya and I communicated only about Yuj now logistical details, drop-offs, pick-ups. Each conversation was a reminder of how far we had drifted, how much space now existed between us.

One evening, I came across an old letter she had written to me, tucked away in a drawer I rarely opened. It was from years ago, back when we were still trying to build a life together.

Kavan,

You make me believe in things I never thought possible. I don't know what the future holds, but with you, it feels like anything is within reach.

I folded the letter carefully, placing it back where I found it. Those words belonged to a different time, a different version of us.

One night, as I sat on the balcony, staring at the city lights, I realized something. I had been holding on not to Radhya, but to the idea of her, the version of her I had built in my mind. And in doing so, I had failed to see who she had become, just as she had failed to see the man I had turned into.

Love wasn't enough because we had stopped growing together. We had stopped listening, stopped trying to understand.

Letting her go wasn't just about accepting the end of us; it was about freeing us both to become who we needed to be, even if that meant walking separate paths.

The next morning, I woke up to Yuj climbing onto my bed, his tiny arms wrapping around my neck.

"Papa," he whispered, "can we go to the park today?"

I kissed his forehead and nodded. "Of course, buddy."

As I got him ready, I felt a strange sense of peace. The pain was still there, raw and unrelenting, but it no longer felt like it was suffocating me. It was a part of me now, a reminder of what we had shared—and what we had lost.

When we reached the park, Yuj ran ahead, his laughter ringing out like a balm to my aching heart. I watched him, a small smile playing on my lips.

Life was moving forward, one step at a time. And so was I.

CHAPTER FOURTEEN

THE DANCE OF HEALING

The morning was quiet, bathed in the soft golden light of dawn. I was having my morning coffee; every sip reminds me of my days and the moments which we perfect now got ruined as the sole thing I love the most was even bland. As I stood at the edge of the hill, overlooking the vast expanse of the city below, there was a stillness within me I hadn't felt in a long time. The air was crisp, fresh, as if it carried the whispers of a new beginning. These are mere my assumptions to make my brain work in the favour of it that this would cherish the upcoming days.

It had been months since everything had changed, since I had been forced to confront the realities of my life, my relationships, my failures. But standing here now, I didn't feel broken. I didn't feel the same weight that had dragged me down for so long. Instead, I felt... Befikr after a very long time.

I had come here to find closure, not just with Radhya, but with myself. And as I looked out over the city, I realized that closure wasn't something someone else could give me. It was something I had to give to myself. Also, there was a seek always in my brain for the closure because it might satisfy my juggle head of emotions.

The past few weeks had been a whirlwind of emotions from acceptance, forgiveness to the slow, painful process of healing. Yuj had gone back to stay with Radhya, and for the first time in a long time, I was alone. Not the suffocating, crushing loneliness I had once feared, but a peaceful solitude. I was learning to be with myself in a way I had never done before.

Hanuman Mandir is now my constant. I started meditating in the mornings, something I had always dismissed as too abstract for me. But now, sitting in silence each day, I found a sense of calm I hadn't known I needed. It wasn't about escaping reality or running from my problems—it was about facing them head-on, acknowledging the pain, and letting it pass through me. It was in those quiet moments that I started to understand what Papa had always tried to teach me, though I hadn't seen it then. His presence wasn't in the grand gestures or the lessons he'd spoken aloud—it was in the small things, the way he carried himself, the way he faced the world with quiet strength and humility. In the way he loved us, without needing to say the words.

Papa had always been my guide, even when he wasn't physically here. And now, I realized, his wisdom was still guiding me—through the silence, through the stillness, through the mess I had made of my life.

One afternoon, I took a long walk through the old neighbourhood it was *Pratap Darwaza*, the place where I had grown up. The streets were familiar, yet distant, like echoes of a past life. I found myself standing outside our old house the one where Papa had raised us, where I had learned to be a man, where I had felt both the weight and the warmth of family.

I closed my eyes and, for a moment, I could hear his voice again. Not in words, but in feeling—in the way the wind whispered through the trees, in the way the earth felt solid beneath my feet. He was here. He had always been here. And in that moment, I realized that I wasn't lost. I was exactly where I needed to be.

The turning point came during a visit to a spiritual retreat at Aloha, something I never would have imagined myself doing. But in the heart of the mountains at Rishikesh, surrounded by strangers seeking their own healing, I felt a connection—both to the people around me and to something far greater than myself.

I met a monk there, a man who had lived a life of quiet reflection, who saw through the layers of pain and confusion I carried with me. We talked for hours, his knowledge in his subjects was immense but it wasn't his words that changed me—it was the way he listened. In his silence, I found answers to questions I hadn't even known I was asking.

"You carry the weight of many things, Kavan," he had said, his voice soft yet firm. **"But the heaviest burden is the one you place on yourself. Let it go. Let yourself be free."**

I didn't understand it at first. But as the days passed, as I spent more time in meditation, reflection, and solitude, I began to see what he meant. My whole routine was now very much in a loop from office to home to meditation. I had been holding on to so much—guilt, regret, fear—things that were no longer serving me. And in clinging to them, I had been holding myself back from the one thing I truly needed: peace.

One evening, back at home, I sat on the balcony, watching the sunset with Yuj on my lap. He was chattering away about school, his friends, and the things he wanted to do over the weekend. His innocence, his joy—it was a reminder of the simplicity of life, of how much beauty there was in the smallest moments.

The learning curve feat. Kavan

I smiled, ruffling his hair. "You know, Yuj," I said quietly, "Life isn't always about being perfect. It's about being present. About loving and learning, and sometimes, letting go."

He looked up at me, his big eyes filled with curiosity. "Like how you love me and Mama?"

I nodded, my heart swelling. "Exactly like that. Love doesn't go away, even when things change."

We sat in silence for a while, watching the sky turn from gold to pink to deep purple. At that moment, I felt a deep sense of gratitude, not just for Yuj, but for everything.

For Radhya, for the lessons I had learned, for the mistakes I had made, and for the man I had become.

The final step in my journey was forgiveness—not just of Radhya, but of myself. We had both made mistakes, we had both caused hurt, but in the end, we had loved each other the best we could. And now, we were finding a new kind of love—one that wasn't about being together, but about being there for Yuj, and for ourselves. We met one evening, just the two of us, to talk. Not about the past, not about blame, but about moving forward. It was the most honest conversation we had ever had. And in the end, we hugged. It wasn't a goodbye, but it was a letting go. A release of all the things that had held us back.

"I'm happy for you," I told her, and I meant it. She smiled, and in her eyes, I saw a reflection of the peace I had found within myself.

As the days turned into weeks, I found myself changing in ways I hadn't expected. The man I had once been driven by ambition, plagued by insecurity was fading away. In his place was someone more grounded, more present, more at peace with the world and with himself.

I had stopped looking for answers outside of myself. I had stopped asking the universe why things were so hard, why life had to be painful. Instead, I started embracing the lessons that life was teaching me. The pain wasn't something to escape—it was something to learn from, to grow from. And in that growth, I found joy. Real, lasting joy. Not in success, not in validation from others, but in the quiet moments—the mornings with Yuj, the conversations with old friends, the stillness of meditation. I had found happiness, not in what I had achieved, but in who I had become.

As I stood in the balcony I felt a sense of completion. The journey had been long, filled with challenges and heartbreak, but it had led me here—to this moment of clarity, of peace, of oneness with myself. The sun was rising now, casting a golden shimmer over the horizon. And as I took a deep breath, I felt a quiet contentment settle within me.

I had found what I was looking for and it was me.

CHAPTER FIFTEEN

MASTERSTROKE: THE FINAL FRAME

Dipanshu stood there with a familiar smile on his face. But this time, Kavan felt something, something he hadn't understood before.

"Ready for the final scene, Kavan?" Dipanshu asked, stepping inside.

Kavan—or rather, **Manhar Khanna**, paused.

The fog of the past months began to lift, revealing a stunning truth. He wasn't Kavan. He was Manhar, the brilliant Actor known for his depth, versatility, and raw talent and this entire time, this journey, this story, had been a directorial masterpiece in the making.

Manhar sat down slowly, the realization washing over him like a wave.

"So... all of this, Kavan's life, Papa, Radhya—it was never real?"

Dipanshu chuckled; his eyes gleaming with satisfaction. It's as real as any great story, Manhar. But it's not yours.

It's Kavan's. I came to you months ago with a proposition, remember? You said you wanted a role that would challenge you like never before.

So, I gave you Kavan—a character whose life would unfold around you, a life you had to live, not just act.

Manhar leaned back, stunned. He remembered the meeting, the brief conversation with Dipanshu where the director had said, this won't be a typical film. You'll live Kavan's journey. At the time, he'd been intrigued but hadn't fully understood what Dipanshu had meant. Now, it all made sense.

"You blurred the line between life and performance," Manhar said slowly, shaking his head in admiration.

Every emotion, every experience—none of it was scripted. I wasn't acting, I was being.

Dipanshu nodded. Exactly. That's why you were perfect for Kavan. You didn't just play a man losing his father, his wife, his sense of self—you became him. You let yourself get lost in the story, so the audience wouldn't just see an actor, they'd see a man unravelling, healing, and growing in real time."

Manhar felt a surge of awe as he looked at Dipanshu. This wasn't just a film. It was a revolutionary approach to storytelling, a blending of reality and narrative that pushed the boundaries of cinema. Kavan's life had felt real because, for a time, it was real—to Manhar, and soon, to the audience.

"Why Kavan? Why this story?" Manhar asked, still trying to wrap his mind around it.

Dipanshu's gaze softened. Because Kavan's story is universal. It's about loss, love, identity, and self-discovery. But I wanted to tell it in a way no one has ever done before. I wanted to give you, and the audience, something raw, something unforgettable. You lived Kavan's life as if it were your own, and when people see it, they'll feel that same immersion.

Manhar felt his pulse quicken. This wasn't just a role; this was something extraordinary. The emotions he had experienced as Kavan—grief for Papa, the unravelling of his relationship with Radhya, the discovery of self in solitude—had all been genuine. And now, as he stood on the other side of it, he realized how deeply he had been transformed by the experience.

"I didn't just play him," Manhar said, his voice quiet. "I was him."

That's the beauty of it, Dipanshu replied, his voice calm but full of conviction. You were Kavan, and when the world sees this, they'll feel every ounce of that truth. It's more than a film, Manhar. It's a life lived on screen.

Manhar stood up, walking to the window, lit up his cig, his mind racing. He had done countless films, taken on challenging roles, but nothing had ever been like this. Dipanshu had crafted a narrative that blurred the boundaries of reality and performance, creating a story that would be impossible to forget.

As he looked out at the fading light, Manhar felt a strange sense of peace. Kavan's story had been painful, beautiful, and transformative, but it was also something more—a reflection of what it meant to be human. And now, it is complete.

He turned back to Dipanshu, a slow smile spreading across his face.

"You were right," he said. "This wasn't just a role. This was the greatest story I've ever been a part of." Dipanshu grinned. "I knew you'd see it that way."

Manhar walked him to the door, feeling lighter, as though a weight had been lifted. "So, what happens next?"

Dipanshu paused at the threshold; his eyes gleaming with satisfaction. "Next? We show the world the life of

Kavan, and they'll realize, just like you did, that it's not about where the story ends. It's about what you become along the way."

Manhar smiled, watching as Dipanshu stepped out. He stood at the door, the same door he had shut behind Dipanshu all those months ago. But now, he understood. This wasn't just the end of a story—it was the start of something much bigger.

As he closed the door, Manhar—no longer Kavan—felt a sense of completion. The narrative had been brilliant, immersive, and unforgettable. And as the real man behind Kavan, he knew this film would leave an indelible mark on everyone who experienced it. All he thanked to Baba.

It was a story for the ages and as an actor, it was the role of a lifetime.

Shukriya

I won't shy away from saying this journey is not just about gratitude toward God, family, friends, and colleagues. It's the realization of a long-orchestrated plan, a manifestation I've worked toward for years. I've spoken about this on countless phone calls, crafted a vision board, and made it a point to check it off my list. And here I am, checking it off—it's a dream come true.

First and foremost, my deepest gratitude goes to Baba Hanumanji, whose constant presence and support have always been my greatest blessing, I really dont know how to thank more. And to my guiding light, Guruji—Shukrana Guruji, Anantum Anantum Shukrana. His power and grace have filled my heart with endless gratitude and joy. I can't thank my family enough for their unwavering support across all my ventures, gigs, and every wild idea that crosses my mind. Their blessings mean everything to me. The more blessings you receive, the more you realize how much you need them. Thank you for always believing in me.

Now, onto the people who've been my gurus/mentors/teachers. They are true gems, always standing by me, guiding and supporting me.

Toast to my very dearest friends who've endured my impromptu speeches, debates, declamations, and endless rants without complaint you all definitely deserve a raise.

I would want to express my sincere appreciation to the Chetanya family for always supporting me and being there for me.

A shoutout to Dhruv Arora, Tushar Verma, Garima and Jiya for helping me in the book journey whenever I need.

Thanks for giving the valuable feedback and inputs regarding book. Definitely, they understood the assignment and outperformed it.

About The Author

Hi, Readers! If you've made it to this page, let me assure you, I won't bore you with clichés or overused introductions. Let me start with a word that resonated with me deeply when I stumbled upon it in 2020—Multipotentialite. It refers to someone with many interests and creative pursuits, and that's exactly who I am.

I'm Naman N; a thinker, dreamer, and storyteller. By profession, I'm a Senior Software Developer, but my passions span far beyond technology. I am also a Language and Soft Skills Instructor, a STEM Facilitator, and a Tarot Card Reader. Over the years, I've crafted a unique blend of intellectual pursuits and spiritual exploration, driven by an insatiable curiosity.

With more than seven years of experience in education and mentoring, I've had the privilege of guiding countless individuals on their journeys of transformation. My approach to teaching is rooted in meaningful connections—whether it's helping students find their voice, inspiring others to embrace uncertainty, or unlocking the mysteries of human behavior through Neuro-Linguistic Programming (NLP). This has been especially rewarding in my work as an IELTS mentor, helping students achieve remarkable results.

An explorer at heart, I embrace every opportunity to venture into new territories. This passion for growth also inspired me to start *Ni:Swarth*, an initiative aimed at supporting underprivileged communities.

I consider myself fortunate for the love and support I've received from those around me, family, friends, students, and everyone who has crossed my path. This love fuels my sense of responsibility and motivates me to spread positivity wherever I can. Of course, I have my flaws and moments of imperfection, but they remind me that I'm human, not a saint.

In this book, I invite you to step into a world of raw emotions, layered relationships, and the hidden struggles that shape us. Each chapter reflects my belief that the best stories are not perfect—they're honest, relatable, and profoundly human.

When I'm not writing, you'll find me seeking inspiration through teaching, traveling, or gazing at the skies, wondering about life's larger purpose. Thank you for joining me on this journey. Let's explore together.

Follow me on instagram **@learn_with_namann :)**

www.ingramcontent.com/pod-product-compliance
Lightning Source LLC
La Vergne TN
LVHW041129150826
845673LV00007B/2240

* 9 7 9 8 8 9 6 3 2 9 4 5 9 *